PRINSESA

Written by
Emmanuel Romero

Story by
Drew Stephens

Illustrated by
Marconi Calindas

First Edition: November 2013 (CS)
ISBN-13: 978-1493647231
ISBN-10: 1493647237

Written by Emmanuel Romero
Story, Layout & Editing by Drew Stephens
Illustrations by Marconi Calindas

Printed in the United States of America

For boys who are really princesses
and girls who are really princes.

The grownups who support these
little ones are true royalty.

Malaya and Jojo live in a cozy blue house with their Mommy and Daddy.

Malaya is 8 years old, and likes dinosaurs.

Jojo is 6 years old, and likes mermaids.

Daddy works at daytime as a mailman, while Mommy works at nighttime as a nurse.

At night, Mommy goes to the hospital to help the sick people feel better, and Daddy stays home with Malaya and Jojo.

Daddy likes to watch baseball games on TV, while Malaya and Jojo play with their toys.

But tonight, something different happened.

There was a big earthquake, and the cozy blue house started shaking.

The hanging lights swung around the ceiling. The books tumbled off the bookshelves. The flower vases tipped over and fell to the floor with a CRASH!

When the house stopped shaking, all the lights had turned off, and it was dark.

Malaya and Jojo were scared of the dark, and cried for Daddy. Daddy found them in their dark bedroom and hugged them.

Daddy lit some candles, and the room glowed orange in the light.

Then he got an idea to make them feel better.

"Do you two want me to tell you a story?"

"Once upon a time," Daddy said, "There was a big, beautiful forest in a land called The Philippines.

There were large rocky mountains, tall, green bamboo trees, and pretty, colorful flowers.

"And dinosaurs?"
asked Malaya.

"Well, we could have dinosaurs if you want,"
Daddy said.

"Nearby lived a young princess. She had long, soft black hair, a silk gown that was pretty like the flowers, and a shiny, shimmering gold fan.

She would go walking in the forest every day. She smelled the fragrant flowers, watched the eagles soar in the sky, and heard the monkeys chatter as they scuttled through the trees.

The forest was her favorite place."

"But one day, when the princess went walking in the forest, there was a great earthquake.

The trees started falling, and the princess was in danger of being trapped."

"A warrior prince was walking nearby. He was a brave man who carried a long sword and a strong wooden shield.

When the earthquake started, he saw the princess in the forest. He ran through the trees to help her."

"The prince found the princess in the forest. The earthquake shook the bamboo trees, sending them crashing to the ground.

But the prince and the princess were not scared. When they saw the trees falling, they moved fast:
TWIST! SPIN! JUMP! HOP!
TWIST! SPIN! JUMP! HOP!
TWIST! SPIN! JUMP! HOP!

It was like the prince and the princess were dancing their way out of the forest."

"After the earthquake was over, the prince and the princess were safe from the trees.

'Thank you for coming to help me,' the princess said to the prince.

'We did it together,' the prince said to the princess. 'You were very brave.'

And the two of them lived happily ever after."

"I like that story, Daddy," said Malaya. "The forest sounded like a fun place."

"The Philippine islands are very beautiful. Maybe we'll visit one day," Daddy said.

"How about you, Jojo? Did you like the story, too?"

"Oh, yes!" Jojo said. "The princess is my favorite."

"Why do you like the princess so much?" Daddy asked.

"Because she is just like me!" Jojo said.

"Don't be silly, Jojo! You're a boy!" said Daddy. "Boys are princes. Only GIRLS are princesses."

"But I want to be the princess!" Jojo said. "I want to wear a pretty gown, have long soft hair, and dance around in the sun! I want to be beautiful!"

Jojo grabbed a pink blanket off Malaya's bed, and wrapped it around like a dress.

Jojo began dancing around the bedroom.

"You look pretty in the candlelight!" Malaya said.

Daddy was confused by Jojo. Jojo was supposed to be a boy, but Jojo wanted to be a princess.

Boys aren't supposed to act like girls, Daddy thought to himself. *If people see my boy acting like a girl, they'll make fun of him.*

What will happen when my friends see Jojo? They won't think I'm a good daddy, and they won't like me or my family anymore.

What will happen in school? If the kids see Jojo acting like a girl, they'll point and laugh, and start whispering naughty words behind his back.

They may even want to start fights with him.

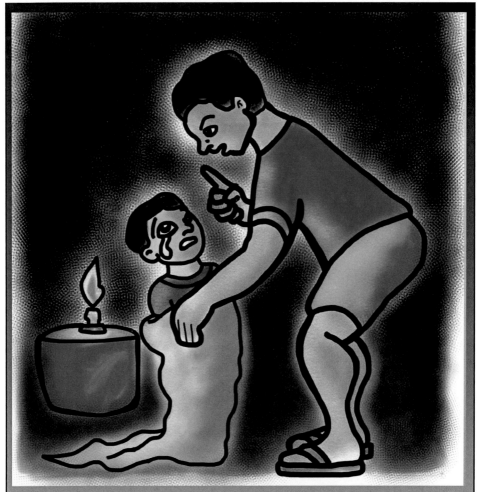

Daddy was very scared about Jojo being a princess. "Jojo, you can't be a princess," he said. "You have to be a prince and act like a boy."

"But I want to be a princess," Jojo said. "I want to be beautiful!"

"Jojo, I said no!" Daddy said in a stern voice.

Jojo became very sad, and started to cry.

Malaya walked over and put her arm around Jojo. "Daddy, why did you make Jojo cry?" Malaya asked. "Why don't you want Jojo to be happy?"

When Malaya asked Daddy that question, it made him think.

Maybe Malaya is right. I love Jojo. I'm Jojo's Daddy. I would rather Jojo act like a princess and be happy, instead of act like a prince and be sad.

Then Daddy started thinking about all the people who would make fun of Jojo.

If people are going to be mean just because Jojo wants to be a princess, I'll have to teach them to be nice. I'll help and protect Jojo from the bad people.

Because I love Jojo. I want Jojo to be happy.

Daddy sat down next to Jojo.

"I was wrong to yell at you, Jojo," Daddy said. "I'm sorry. You can be a princess if you want. I love you, and I want you to be happy."

Jojo stopped crying and hugged Daddy.

Malaya came over and took them both by the hand, and they all started dancing together.

Later that night, the lights flickered back on in the house. Mommy came back from the hospital.

Malaya and Jojo came running from the bedroom, and they were both wearing pretty dresses and paper crowns.

"Wow!" Mommy said. "We don't have one, but two princesses!"

"Yes we do," Daddy said. "They're both very pretty, and very brave."

The two children tell Mommy the story about the beautiful forest in the Philippines, where there were two princesses:

Princess Malaya
and
Princess Jojo

The End

EMMANUEL ROMERO - cut his teeth as a creative writer at Bindlestiff Studio, the only permanent community-based creative arts center for Filipino Americans in the U.S. He studied stand-up comedy under Kevin Camia, wrote and performed with sketch comedy group Taste Better Wit, and was a contributing writer to The Bakla Show in 2007 and 2010. One of his single-act plays, *"Viewer Discretion Advised (Tape 96),"* was adapted into an award-winning short film.

"To Ray, Alex and Abel Romero Rubio: Tito Emm loves you like a pink tutu!"

MARCONI CALINDAS - Marconi is an award-winning San Francisco LGBT artist, a grand prize winner for the 2012 New Era Introducing Global Creative Project North America which his winning piece toured in five key art cities in North America: New York City, Miami, Los Angeles, Chicago and Toronto, Canada.

Marconi was recognized with a Certificate of Honor by the San Francisco City Hall Office of Supervisors for his triumph. Marconi also is a runner-up for the 2013 Details Magazine Future of Social Media Art Contest. His LGBT themed and island inspired art has been showcased in San Francisco City Hall, the Children's Creative Museum, Hotel Triton Mezzanine Gallery, Magnet SF and at Menlo College. He also has had notable exhibits at A-Forest Gallery in NYC, Intermedia Arts Gallery in Minneapolis, Artists Alley San Francisco, and Aspect Gallery in San Francisco among many others.

For more info visit WWW.MARCONICALINDAS.COM.

DREW STEPHENS - is an award-winning filmmaker, published author and internationally-acclaimed television and radio producer. Drew was the original host & segment producer for Electric City LGBT TV in San Francisco, and a pioneering member of IBC-TV in Thailand.

Drew sends love to his family and friends for their undying support, especially to Mano, his husband of 22 years, for allowing him to spoil his own inner child.

PRINSESA

Did you like this story? Watch the movie!

"Prinsesa" is also a short film!
Featuring the work of over 40 volunteers, including:
Scary Cow Film Productions
Likha Pilipino Folk Ensemble
Bindlestiff Studio
and more!

WWW.PRINSESAFILM.COM

Questions about gender identity or bullying?
Some great places to start:

TransActive:
WWW.TRANSACTIVEONLINE.ORG

PFLAG Transgender Network:
HTTP://TINYURL.COM/PFLAG-T

Stop Bullying:
WWW.STOPBULLYING.GOV

Made in the USA
San Bernardino, CA
21 November 2018